JUV/E
FIC
Novak, Matt.

While the
   shepherd slept.

$13.95

DATE	BORROWER'S NAME	
0-91		

Matt Novak

While the Shepherd Slept

Orchard Books · New York

Orchard Books, A division of Franklin Watts, Inc., 387 Park Avenue South, New York, NY 10016

Manufactured in the United States of America. Printed by General Offset Co., Inc. Bound by Horowitz / Rae.
The text of this book is set in 18 pt. Weiss Bold. The illustrations are colored pencil.
Book design by Mina Greenstein.   10   9   8   7   6   5   4   3   2   1

Library of Congress Cataloging-in-Publication Data
Novak, Matt. While the shepherd slept / by Matt Novak.   p.   cm.
Summary: While the shepherd sleeps, the sheep sneak away to perform in a vaudeville show.
ISBN 0-531-05915-4.   ISBN 0-531-08515-5 (lib.)
[1. Sheep—Fiction.   2. Sleep—Fiction.]   I. Title.   PZ7.N867Wh   1991   [E]—dc20   90-7733   CIP   AC

To Bob

*E*very morning the shepherd was tired.
But the sheep didn't mind one bit.

When he fell asleep, as he did every afternoon,
the sheep quietly sneaked away.

They nibbled their way to town
and arrived at the theater.

"Hurry! Hurry!" the theater manager called.

"You're late! You're late!" the wardrobe mistress cried.

"You're on! You're on!" the director shouted.

The curtain rose,

and the audience cheered.

There were funny skits

and sad songs.

There was breathtaking suspense

and loud applause.

When the show was over, the sheep took their bows.

Then they folded their costumes and packed them away.

"Be on time tomorrow!" the theater manager said.

The sheep nibbled their way back to the hills

and arrived just as the shepherd was waking.
"You are all so good," he said. "You never wander."

He led the sheep to the warm barn,
where they soon fell asleep.

Then the shepherd went to town,

where he danced until dawn.

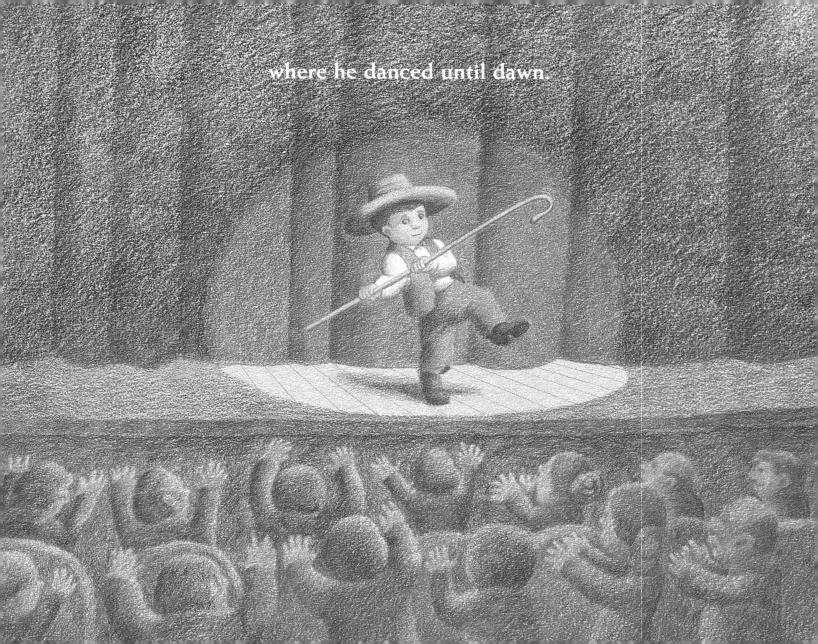

WHILE THE SHEPHERD SLEPT